The Ladybird Key Words Reading Scheme is based on these commonly used words. Those used most often in the English language are introduced first—with other words of popular appeal to children. All the Key Words list is covered in the early books, and the later titles use further word lists to develop full reading fluency. The total number of different words which will be learned in the complete reading scheme is nearly two thousand. The gradual introduction of these words, frequent repetition and complete 'carry-over' from book to book, will ensure rapid learning.

The full colour illustrations have been designed to create a desirable attitude towards learning— by making every child *eager* to read each title. Thus this attractive reading scheme embraces not only the latest findings in word frequency, but also the natural interests and activities of happy children.

Each book contains a list of the new words introduced.

W MURRAY, the author of the Ladybird Key Words Reading Scheme, is an experienced headmaster, author and lecturer on the teaching of reading. He is co-author, with J McNally, of Key Words to Literacy — *a teacher's book published by The Teacher Publishing Co Ltd.*

THE LADYBIRD KEY WORDS READING SCHEME has 12 graded books in each of its three series—'**a**', '**b**' and '**c**'. As explained in the handbook *Teaching Reading*, these 36 graded books are all written on a controlled vocabulary, and take the learner from the earliest stages of reading to reading fluency.

The '**a**' series gradually introduces and repeats new words. The parallel '**b**' series gives the needed further repetition of these words at each stage, but in a different context and with different illustrations.

The '**c**' series is also parallel to the '**a**' series, and supplies the necessary link with writing and phonic training.

An illustrated booklet—*Notes for using the Ladybird Key Words Reading Scheme*—can be obtained free from the publishers. This booklet fully explains the Key Words principle. It also includes information on the reading books, work books and apparatus available, and such details as the vocabulary loading and reading ages of all books.

BOOK 3a
The Ladybird Key Words Reading Scheme

Things we like

by W. MURRAY

with illustrations by MARTIN AITCHISON

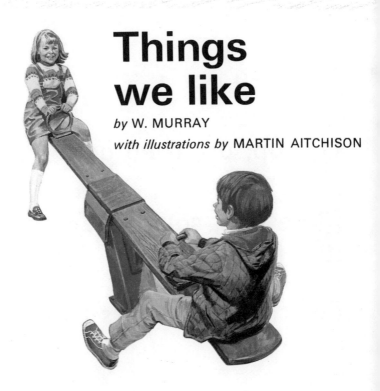

Ladybird Books Loughborough

Here are Peter and Jane.

They like to play.

Up they go.

Up, up, up, they go.

I like this, says Peter.
It is fun.

Pat the dog wants to play.

---

new words

play   up

Jane and Peter like
to play.

Here they are at play.

I go up, up, up, says Jane.

I go down, down, down,
says Peter.

Up and down, up and down,
up and down we go.

new words

at   down

Jane and Peter play
in the water.

They like to play
on the boat.

Come on, says Peter.

Come on the boat.

Come and play on the boat.

Jump up.   Jump up here.

new words

on   boat

Jane is in the water and Peter is in the boat.

They want to fish.

Peter can see a fish in the water.

Get in the boat, says Peter.

The fish can see you in the water.

Get in the boat, Jane.

---

new words

see   Get   get

Look at me, says Peter.

Look at me, Jane.

Look at me in the boat.

Come on, he says.

Come and play in the boat, Jane.

Come on, Pat.

---

new word

me

Here is the station.

Peter and Jane are at the station.

They like the station.

The train comes in.

Look at the train, says Peter.

See the train, Jane.

I like trains, he says.

New words

station   train

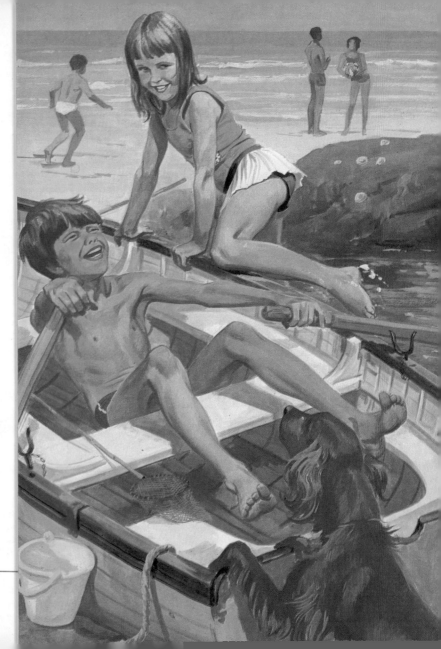

I want a cake, please,
says Peter.

A cake for me, please,
he says.

Here you are, says Jane.

Here are some cakes.

A cake for you and
a cake for me.

I like cakes and you like
cakes.

new words

cake   please

Peter likes to play
with toys.

He plays with a toy station
and a toy train.

Jane says, Please can I play?

Please can I play with you?

Yes, says Peter. I have
the train.

You play with the station.

---

new word

with

Here is the shop.

Peter and Jane look at
the dogs.

They look at the rabbits.

Look at this one,
says Peter.

This is the one we want.

Yes, this is the one.

We want this rabbit.

---

new words

rabbits   one

Peter and Jane go into the shop.

We want that rabbit, says Peter to the man.

Yes, that one, please.

Here you are, says the man.

Here it is, he says.

new words

that   man

Jane and Peter like to help Mummy.

They go to the shops for Mummy.

I like to shop, says Jane. It is fun.

Come on, Peter says. We have to go to the fish shop.

Yes, says Jane. It helps Mummy.

---

new words

help   Mummy

Peter and Jane like to help Daddy.

They help Daddy with the car.

Jane is in the car.

Daddy and Peter have some water.

Peter likes to play with water.

I like it, he says. It is fun.

---

new words

Daddy   car

Here they go, in the car.

Daddy is in the car with Peter and Jane.

We like it in the car, they say.

Go on, Daddy, go on.

We want to go on and on.

This is good fun, they say.

---

new word

good

Look, Jane, that is a
Police car.

It says POLICE on it.

That is the Police Station.

I like the Police, says Peter.
They help you.

Yes, says Jane. The Police
help you.

---

new words

Police   POLICE

Here is an apple tree.

Apples are good for you,
says Peter.

Have an apple, Jane.

An apple for you and
an apple for me.

Mummy wants some and
we want some.

No, Pat, no apples for you.

---

new words

an   apple

Peter and Jane are at home.

They play with the rabbit.

They like to see the rabbit jump.

Give it an apple, says Peter.

No, says Jane. Give it some water.

The man in the shop says it wants water.

---

new words

Give   give

Here are some trees and flowers.

Jane and Peter want some flowers.

Some flowers for you and some for me, says Jane.

Get some flowers, Peter.

Get some for Mummy and get some for Daddy.

---

new word

flowers

The man in the shop likes Jane and Peter, and they like the man.

He has the apples they like.

We want the red ones, please, they say.

Get the red ones, please.

---

new word

red

Peter has the red ball.

He plays with the boys
with the red ball.

Jane looks on.

That was good, Peter, says
Jane. That was good.

The boys say, Yes, Peter,
that was good.

Good for you.

---

new words

boys   was

See the bus, Peter.

See the red bus.

The boys and the girls are in the bus.

Come on, Peter, says Jane.

We have to get in.

The boys and the girls like the bus.

It is fun in the bus.

---

new words

bus   girls

44

The boys and girls
go to school.

They go to school
in the bus.

The boys and girls like to
go to school in the bus.

They have fun in the bus.

They like the bus and
they like school.

---

new word

school

Some boys and girls come to tea.

They come to tea with Jane and Peter.

Jane helps Mummy with the tea.

Jane gives the girls tea, and Peter gives the boys cakes.

They like to have boys and girls to tea.

---

new word

tea

48

Up to bed, Jane,
says Mummy.

Up to bed, Peter,
says Daddy.

Up to bed you go.

Yes, say Peter and Jane.
We want to go to bed.

It was fun in the water,
says Peter.

Yes, says Jane, and it
was fun at tea.

---

new word

bed

a rabbit

a boat

an apple

a cake

a car

the red bus

a man

the school

some boys

some girls

the train

a bed

some flowers

a boat

a rabbit

an apple

a cake

a car

a man

the red bus

some boys

the school

some girls

the train

a bed

some flowers

New words used in this book

Total number of new words 36